MY MAMA NEEDS ME

by
Mildred Pitts Walter
pictures by Pat Cummings

· LOTHROP, LEE & SHEPARD BOOKS/NEW YORK ·

Library of Congress Cataloging in Publication Data. Walter, Mildred Pitts. My mama needs me. Summary: Jason wants to help, but isn't sure that his mother needs him at all after she brings home a new baby from the hospital. [1. Babies —Fiction.   2. Mother and child—Fiction]   I. Cummings, Pat, ill.   II. Title.   PZ7.W17125My   1983   [E]   82-12654
ISBN 0-688-01670-7   ISBN 0-688-01671-5   (lib. bdg.)

For Jason, Shanika, and Nizam
—M.P.W.

For Artie
—P.C.

Jason's friends rushed over to see the new baby,
just home from the hospital.
"Sh, sh-h-h, she's sleeping," Jason said.
"Hey, Jason, want to come play?" Terry asked.
"Can't. The baby's home."
"How come you can't play?" Craig asked.
"I just told you."
"So?" Jonathan said.
"So, my mama needs me."

Jason rushed inside.
"Can I hold her?"
he asked his mama.
"Not now.
When she wakes up,"
his mama said.
His father went back to work.
His mama went to bed.
Jason watched the baby.
She slept and slept and slept.

Jason went into his backyard.
He started up when Mrs. Luby called over the fence,
"Hi, Jason. Come have some cookies and milk with me."
Jason slipped through the back gate.
Mrs. Luby uncovered a plate of spicy brown cookies
and poured cold milk.
Jason reached for a cookie. Suddenly he stopped.
What if my little sister wakes up, he thought.
"No, Mis' Luby. I can't stay.
My mama needs me."

Inside his house, he tiptoed
to his mama's room and listened.
No sound.
He quietly opened the door. "Ma. Ma!
You want me to do something?"
"Please, Jason. Just let me sleep."
"Only wanted to help," he mumbled.
He went back outside.
He thought of the cold milk
and the spicy brown cookies.
But Mrs. Luby was no longer in
her yard.

Jason sat on the back steps. He heard the hum of the city. He heard his friends playing ball. But there was only silence in his house. *Nobody needs me,* he said to himself. *I need something to do!*

Suddenly he heard an unfamiliar noise. It was his little sister crying! His heart beat wildly as he rushed inside. "Why is she crying?" he asked.

"She's hungry," his mama said.

"Can I help feed her?"

"She gets her milk from my breast."

His mama lay back on the bed to feed the baby.

The baby could hardly wait.
Her little hands beat the air. Her little body wiggled.
Jason watched the baby snuggle to the breast.
Soon she was quiet. In no time at all she was asleep again.
Mama rubbed the top of the baby's ear.
The baby stirred and started nursing. Jason laughed.
But right away she was sleeping again.
Jason rubbed the top of the tiny ear
the way his mother had done.
The baby wiggled and really started nursing.
Mama laughed with Jason and said,
"She likes your touch."

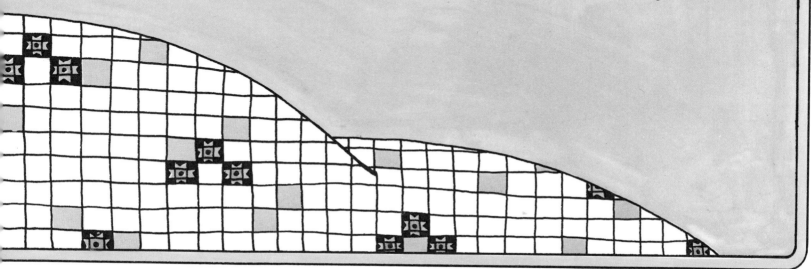

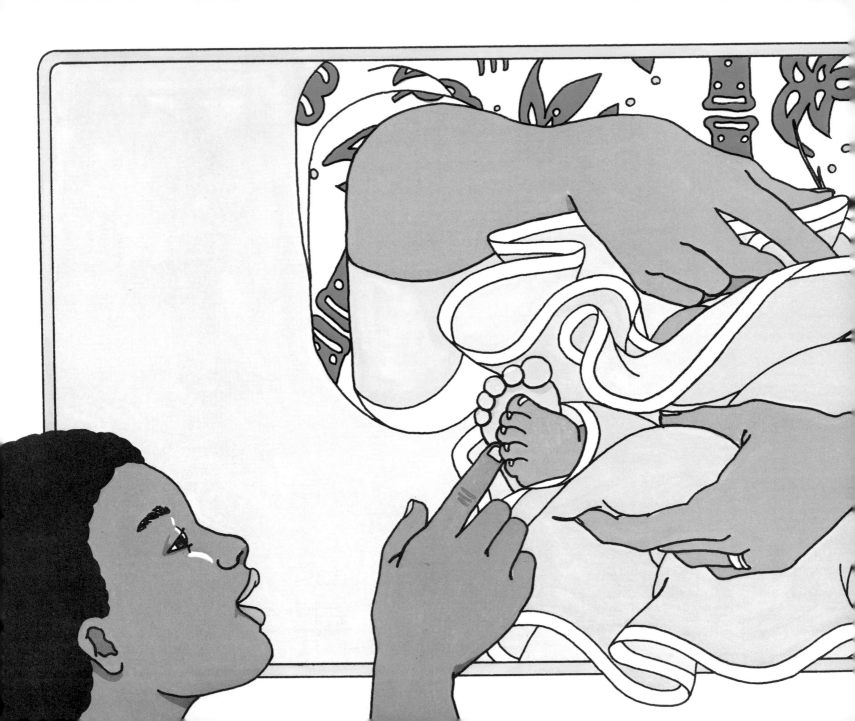

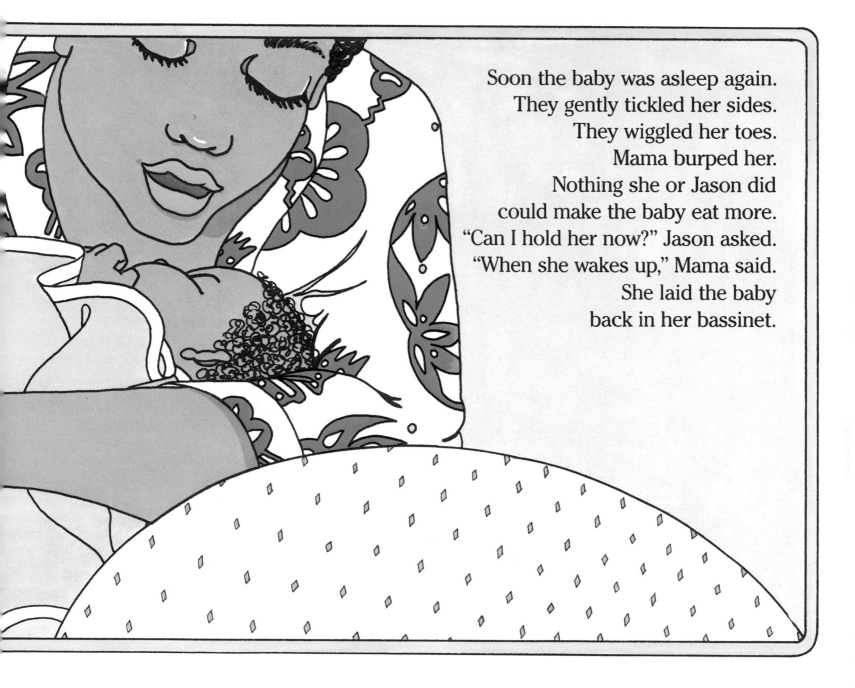

Soon the baby was asleep again.
They gently tickled her sides.
They wiggled her toes.
Mama burped her.
Nothing she or Jason did
could make the baby eat more.
"Can I hold her now?" Jason asked.
"When she wakes up," Mama said.
She laid the baby
back in her bassinet.

Jason followed his mama to the kitchen.
She took a chicken out of the freezer.
"Are we going to make dinner?"
"Not now. I'm going to rest a while longer."
Was she that tired when I was born?
Jason wondered.
Again he thought of Mrs. Luby and the cookies.
Maybe he should go find his friends.
They wanted him!

He wandered outside.
Just then, Mr. Pompey, a neighbor, came along.
He was on his way to feed ducks at the pond.
"Hi, Jason. Want to come feed the ducks today?"
Should he go? Jason thought of the quiet house.
Then he thought about the baby. *She won't wake up.*
He would go and feed the ducks.

"Can I carry the bread?" he asked Mr. Pompey.
"Think you're strong enough for that?"
"It's only bread!" Jason said.
Mr. Pompey laughed and handed him the loaf.
As Jason walked beside his friend,
he tried to step on his own shadow.
The pond was quiet.
Mr. Pompey made a loud quacking sound,
and the ducks on the pond headed toward shore.
Some swam gracefully.
Some raised their wings
and moved like skiers on the water.

The quacking ducks crowded around Jason.
Suddenly he thought about his little sister
and quickly handed the bread to Mr. Pompey.
"Open it. Give it to the ducks," Mr. Pompey said.
"I can't. I've got to go. My mama needs me."

After Mr. Pompey brought him home, Jason waited.
Still nothing but silence. *Why do babies sleep so much?*
Sleep, cry, eat, and then sleep some more.
I should have stayed at the pond, he said to himself.
Finally his mama called, "Jason, Jason, where are you?"
"I'm coming, Ma," he said, and rushed inside.

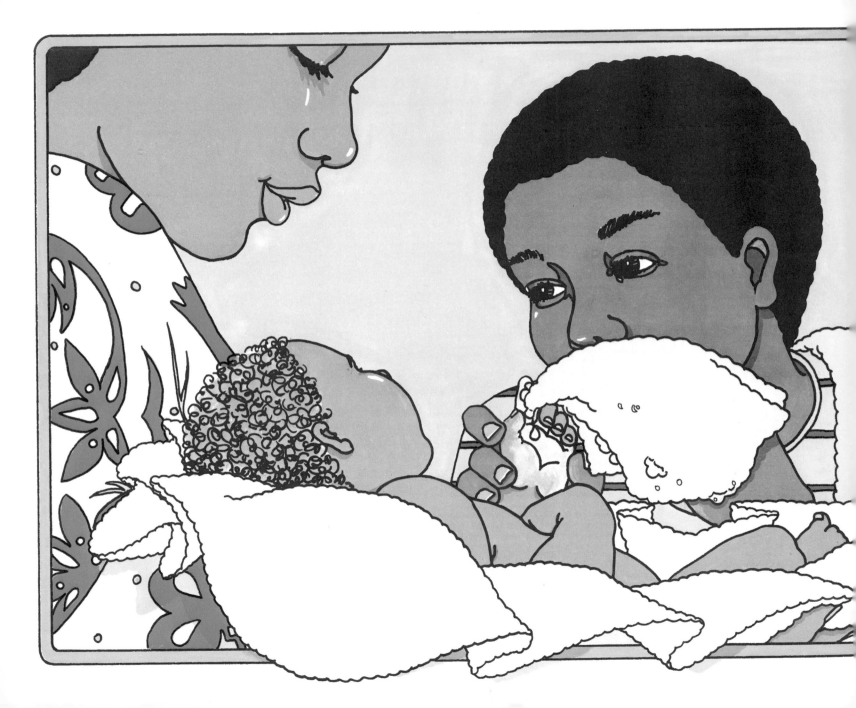

"We're going to bathe the baby now. You can help."
Jason's hands trembled with excitement as he chose
the baby's clothes. He got the soap.
He got the oil and the powder.
He helped wash her soft body, and he helped pat her dry,
very gently. Soon she was dressed and wide awake.
"Can I hold her *now*?"
"If you sit down," his mama said.

Baby Oil

With a pillow on his lap, Jason held his little sister.
All too soon she was fast asleep, and back in her bassinet.
"You are a good helper," his mama said.
"But why don't you go and find your friends?"
"Because. You . . . don't you need me?"
"Of course I need you. I need a big hug from you right now.
I love you, but that doesn't mean
you can't go play with your friends."
Jason gave his mama a warm hug.
That's what I needed to do, he thought.
He was so happy he hugged her again.
Then he waved good-bye and went out to play with his friends.

206739